OLIVER & PATCH

FOR LOU, LAUREN,
JAKE AND TOM
KH

SIMON AND SCHUSTER
First published in Great Britain in 2015 by Simon and Schuster UK Ltd, 1st Floor, 222 Gray's Inn Road, London WC1X 8HB • A CBS Company • Text copyright © 2015 Claire Freedman
Illustrations copyright © 2015 Kate Hindley • The right of Claire Freedman and Kate Hindley to be identified as the author and illustrator of this work has been asserted by them in
accordance with the Copyright, Designs and Patents Act, 1988 • All rights reserved, including the right of reproduction in whole or in part in any form • A CIP catalogue record for this
book is available from the British Library upon request. • 978-0-85707-953-4 (HB) • 978-1-47114-507-0 (PB) • 978-1-47112-264-4 (eBook) • Printed in China • 10 9 8 7 6 5 4 3 2

OLIVER AND PATCH

CLAIRE FREEDMAN AND KATE HINDLEY

LIAM
NDER DOG

LOST
ROVER

SIMON AND SCHUSTER
London New York Sydney Toronto New Delhi

Oliver had just moved to the big city. It felt strange, and his old home in the countryside seemed far, far away.

"I miss the green fields," Oliver sighed. "I miss the wide open spaces. Most of all, I miss my friends."

One morning, Oliver felt restless. Even though the rain was pouring
down like silver needles, he wanted to be outside, to explore.
People hurried by, un-seeing and un-looking.

Oliver glanced about, wondering which way to go, when suddenly
he saw it, bright as a poppy in a cornfield . . .

. . . a small, soggy, white ball of a dog, trailing a streak of red leash.

He was all alone, just like Oliver.

"Hello!" said Oliver. "Are you lost?"

He looked at the little dog's collar tag. Patch, it read. Just Patch.

Oliver looked around.

No one was calling for their little lost dog.

"What shall I do with you?" Oliver said to Patch.
"I can't leave you on your own."

Before he knew it, Oliver had the lead in his hand and Patch was trotting along beside him.

Oliver and Patch had a wonderful day
getting to know each other.

For the first time since moving to the city, Oliver felt happy.

But as dusk fell, Patch became
sad. He sat on Oliver's desk
by the window and gazed out
longingly.

Somewhere out there,
in the rain-hazy twinkle
of the city night lights,
was his real home.

Oliver woke the next morning
to scratchy, scuffling noises.
"Oh, Patch!" Oliver laughed.

They played all day long.

Hide and seek!

Tickle tummy!

Bury the biscuit!

Curl up and cuddle!
(Their favourite.)

Watering the garden –
oops!

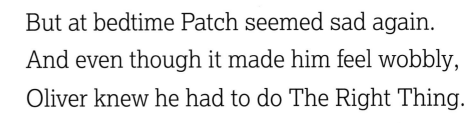

But at bedtime Patch seemed sad again.
And even though it made him feel wobbly,
Oliver knew he had to do The Right Thing.

So the next day he made some posters.

He secretly hoped no one
would see them.

FOUND
SMALL WHITE DOG CALLED PATCH
LIKES CHEWING CUSHIONS
LOVES ANYTHING THE COLOUR RED
DOES SOMERSAULTS
TELEPHONE OLIVER 1234 56789

He stuck up the posters and asked at some shops and houses.

"No, never seen that dog before," the shopkeepers said.

"No one I know is missing a dog," said his neighbours.

Days slipped by and nobody called.

Oliver began to believe that Patch would be his dog forever.

He bought him a cosy red blanket and lots of toys.

It was as if they had
always been friends.

One morning, it was gently drizzling.
Oliver and Patch went exploring.
They wandered down a narrow street,
past tall iron railings by an ancient church.
Suddenly, Patch barked.
He tugged hard on the lead and broke free.

"Patch!" Oliver called.
"PATCH!"

Breathless, Oliver reached a tiny park, hidden away like
a jewel. A girl was sitting on the swings, sad and alone.
Oliver looked at her red coat and red boots – and he knew.

The little girl was hugging Patch. Hugging and hugging.
Oliver tried to be brave, but his world had turned grey again.
"Hello, I'm Ruby," the girl said, smiling at Oliver.
"Have you been looking after Patch for me?"

"It's been lovely," said Oliver, trying hard to smile back.
"But I'm really going to miss him."
Then he had a thought. "Ruby, do you think – maybe –
you and Patch would like to visit me one day?"

"We'd love to!" said Ruby. "But why don't we go and do something together – right now?"

"Woof!" barked Patch. "Woof woof!"

Oliver and Ruby laughed.

At that moment the sun burst out. The pavements shone as a million raindrops glistened like gold. The city looked beautiful.

And Oliver realised he hadn't lost a friend . . .

. . . he had found another one!